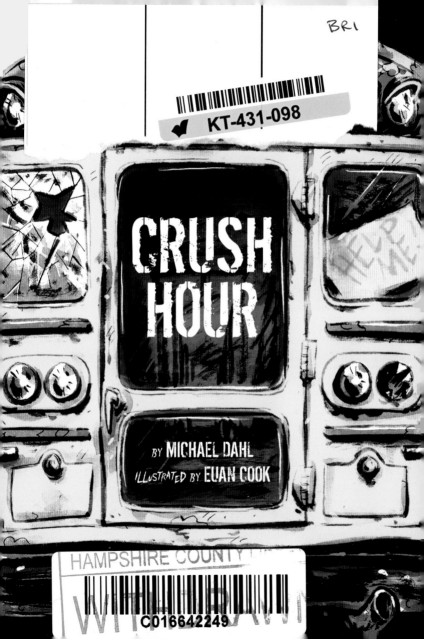

BRI

KT-431-098

CRUSH
HOUR

BY MICHAEL DAHL

ILLUSTRATED BY EUAN COOK

Raintree is an imprint of Capstone Global Library Limited, a company incorporated in England and Wales having its registered office at 264 Banbury Road, Oxford, OX2 7DY – Registered company number: 6695582

www.raintree.co.uk
myorders@raintree.co.uk

Designed by Bob Lentz
Original illustrations © Capstone Global Library Limited 2019
Design element: Cover background by Shutterstock/oldmonk
Production by Tori Abraham
Originated by Capstone Global Library Ltd
Printed and bound in India

ISBN 978 1 4747 5932 8
22 21 20 19 18
10 9 8 7 6 5 4 3 2 1

British Library Cataloguing in Publication Data
A full catalogue record for this book is available from the British Library.

CONTENTS

From dawn to dusk, the **SCHOOL BUS OF HORRORS** rumbles along city streets and down country roads, searching for another passenger. Yellow, black markings, dirty windows – it looks like any other school bus.

But **BEWARE!** Step aboard this bus and experience the scariest ride of your life . . .

CHAPTER ONE
THE VERY BACK

Ella always sits in the seats at the back of the bus.

All by herself.

Alone.

Ella hates feeling crowded. She hates touching other people.

"People are gross!" she always says to herself.

At the back of the bus, Ella has more room.

No one can touch her.

Ella clutches her bag to her chest.

Her seat is greasy. The windows are smudged with dirt.

This is not her usual bus.

The other driver must be off sick, she thinks.

Ella hears a deep voice.

"Ella . . . is this yours?"

The strange bus driver waves a notebook at her.

A grimy plastic wall surrounds the driver's seat.

The driver's wrinkled hand sticks
out from a small opening in the wall.

"You dropped it on the steps,"
croaks the driver.

Ella walks slowly towards the front of the bus.

She feels strange as she stares at the notebook.

It is her journal.

CHAPTER TWO
THE WRINKLED HAND

Ella always keeps the journal
on her bedside table.

How did it get here? she wonders.

Ella grabs the notebook from
the driver.

She is careful not to touch his wrinkled hand.

"Those fingers look gross," she tells herself. "I'll have to wipe off the book when I get to school."

REEEEEERRRRRRRKKKK!

A grinding noise fills the bus.

The passengers turn and look towards the back of the bus.

The back seat – the seat Ella was sitting in – has moved.

The bus is one row shorter!

The back seat has been pushed forward. It has been smashed into the next row of seats.

"AHHHH!" kids scream.

They scramble away from the back of the bus.

They crawl over the seats and rush towards the front of the bus.

As the other kids move forward, Ella steps back.

"Don't touch me!" she says.

No one can hear her over another grinding sound.

REEEEEERRRRRRKKKK!

CHAPTER THREE

Ella and the other kids stand frozen. They stare at the back of the bus.

The back of the bus slowly moves forward.

The last three rows of seats are crushed into each other.

"Let us out!" scream the kids.

The bus keeps moving along the street towards school.

The driver behind the thick plastic wall chuckles.

"We have to get off!" Ella shouts. **"NOW!"**

Each time the bus passes another street, it gets shorter.

More and more kids squeeze into
the front of the bus.

They pound on the dirty windows.
They bang their hands against the
locked door.

REEEEEERRRRRRRKKKK!

The bus is squeezed again. Only one row of seats remains.

All the kids are crowded together like pickled onions in a jar.

The hands and knees and feet of other kids crush into Ella's sides.

CHAPTER FOUR
THE FINAL SQUEEZE

Ella's ears fill with the screams and shouts of the other passengers.

Then the bus stops suddenly.

Ella takes a deep breath to scream once more.

Maybe the bus driver will finally hear her.

"*LET ME OUT!*"

The doors open with a rush of air.

The bus has arrived at school.

Ella and the other kids fall out onto the ground. They tumble like sweets from a ripped bag.

Ella lays on the ground, unable to stand up.

"Do you need help?" asks a voice.

A girl is standing over her.

The girl reaches out and grabs Ella's hand. She helps Ella to her feet.

"I think this is your notebook," says the girl.

She hands Ella the journal. Two words are scribbled on the last page.

"You're welcome," Ella reads the words aloud.

She looks back. The strange bus is a normal size again.

Ella shivers with fear as she watches the bus door creak shut.

But she does not let go as the other girl squeezes her hand.

GLOSSARY

grimy covered by a build-up of dirt or soot

gross ugly or disgusting

journal diary in which someone writes down thoughts and experiences

remains something that is left over

scramble rush or struggle to get somewhere

smudged messy

surround be on every side of something

tumble fall suddenly and helplessly

DISCUSS

1. Why do you think this book is called *Crush Hour*?

2. How do you think Ella's journal got on the bus? What are some other possibilities?

3. Do you think the bus journey was a good or bad experience for Ella? Use examples from the story to support your answer.

WRITE

1. Create a new title for this book. Then write a paragraph on why you chose your new title.

2. Write your own short story about a character getting stuck in a tight space. How does he or she get out?

3. Write about the scariest bus journey you've ever experienced.

AUTHOR

MICHAEL DAHL is the author of the Library of Doom series, the Dragonblood books and Michael Dahl's Really Scary Stories. (He wants everyone to know that last title was not his idea.) He was born a few minutes after midnight of April Fool's Day in a thunderstorm, has survived various tornados and hurricanes, as well as an attack from a rampant bunny at night ("It reared up at me!"). He currently lives in a haunted house and once saw a ghost in his high school. He will never travel on a school bus. These stories will explain why.

ILLUSTRATOR

EUAN COOK is an illustrator from London, who enjoys drawing pictures for books and watching foxes and jays out of his window. He also likes walking around looking at broken brickwork, sooty statues and the weird drainpipes and stuff you can find behind old run-down buildings.

SCHOOL BUS OF HORRORS